This Book Belongs To:

The Muppet Babies live in a nursery
in a house on a street that is a lot like yours.
But they can travel anywhere anytime using a special power—
the power of the imagination.
Can you imagine what it would be like to go with them?
Join the Muppet Babies on this adventure and find out.

Weekly Reader Presents

Baby Gonzo's Unfinished Dream

By Joanne Barkan • Illustrated by Tom Cooke

Muppet Press • New York

This book is a presentation of
Weekly Reader Books.

Weekly Reader Books offers book clubs for children
from preschool through high school.

For further information write to:
Weekly Reader Books
4343 Equity Drive
Columbus, Ohio 43228

Weekly Reader is a trademark of Field Publications.

Printed in the United States of America

It was nap time. For almost an hour, the quiet sounds of sleep filled the nursery. Then suddenly—

"I've got you! You're *it!*"

Baby Gonzo sat up in bed, eyes wide open and nose twitching. A dream had awakened him, and all the noise he made had awakened the other Muppet Babies, too.

"Galloping grannies!" whooped Gonzo. "That was one of my greatest dreams ever. I was playing tag with the jelly bean Martians—me against all of them. I had just tagged a purple one, so they were *it*. Now, that's what I call exciting."

"I was having a wonderful dream, too," sniffed Piggy.
"I was in the most beautiful dress shop in the world, and I
was about to try on a long ball gown and a matching cape
—and then you woke me up."

Kermit yawned and stretched. "I was riding a sailfish
across a blue lake. Whoosh! We were flying!"

"What happens to all the dreams that aren't finished?" asked Gonzo. "They can't just fizzle away. I want to get back to mine and play some more tag."

"Gee," said Kermit, "I never thought about that before. Maybe they go to a kind of dream junk yard."

Piggy frowned. "My unfinished dreams are not junk."

"Well, maybe it's more like a flea market," suggested Kermit. "Nanny told me about flea markets. They sell all sorts of old things and used things."

Piggy stood up. "Let's stop talking about junk and fleas. It's time for our snack. We'll have a tea party. Dreaming makes me very hungry."

All the Babies got ready for their snack, except Gonzo. He sat where he was, thinking about what Kermit had said.

"A flea market for unfinished dreams," he whispered. "That's it. That's where I'll find mine."

Gonzo blinked...

...*AND THERE HE WAS.* He was standing beneath a large gateway. The sign on the gateway read:

FLEA MARKET
OLD, USED, AND UNFINISHED DREAMS
SEE OWNER: FELICIA FLEA

"This is the place," said Gonzo. He stepped through the gateway and set off to find the owner of the market.

"Felicia Flea?" Gonzo politely addressed the tidy-looking flea who was sitting next to the cash register.

The flea nodded her head and stared at Gonzo with glittering green eyes. "I'll bet you're looking for an unfinished dream," she said in a clear voice. She pointed to the left. "Walk to the far end of the market, and you'll find the unfinished dream bottles."

Then, with the wink of a flea, Felicia added, "Here's some flea advice. If you don't have a friend with you, at least take a friend's dream. It's the next best thing."

Gonzo turned to the left and walked through the market. He passed rows and rows of tables piled high with bits of memories and strings of wishes, old and new. There were boxes of big hopes, bags of little ones, and tall, covered jars filled with silly ideas.

Gonzo looked it all over as he walked by. "So this is the stuff dreams are made of," he murmured.

When Gonzo reached the far side of the market, he found a long table covered with bottles. Each bottle contained one unfinished dream.

"Here's mine!" Gonzo shouted as he picked up a bottle filled with dots of color. "And here's Kermit's dream, and this one is Piggy's."

Gonzo carried the three bottles over to a quiet spot just beyond the market. He took a deep breath, pulled the cork out of his own dream bottle, and—

VROOOSH and KAZOOOM! He was back in his dream.
"Hurray!" shouted Gonzo. "It's time for more tag!
Here come the jelly bean Martians, and they're *it!*"
Gonzo turned and started running across a field and up
a low hill. He ran as fast as he could, but the Martians
began to catch up.

Gonzo hadn't forgotten Felicia's flea advice. "Maybe Kermit's dream can help me," he panted. "After all, in dream tag, you can do *anything* that's fun." Gonzo stopped to pull the cork out of Kermit's bottle.

VROOOSH and KAZOOOM! Gonzo was suddenly standing at the edge of a large blue lake. A sleek silver sailfish emerged from the water.

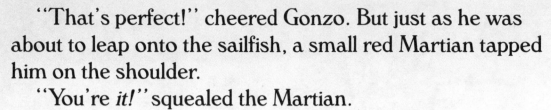

"That's perfect!" cheered Gonzo. But just as he was about to leap onto the sailfish, a small red Martian tapped him on the shoulder.

"You're *it!*" squealed the Martian.

The jelly bean Martians jumped into the lake, and as they did, water skis appeared on their strange, little feet. Then off they went, leaving behind a trail of foam.

"Here I come," yelled Gonzo.

The sailfish whisked Gonzo across the water. But when he reached the far shore, most of the Martians had hopped out of the lake. Gonzo lunged forward. He stretched his arm as far as he could. He managed to touch the last Martian. "You're *it!*" he shouted.

Gonzo was too out of breath to run anymore. So he held up Piggy's dream bottle. "Now another friend comes in handy," he said as he pulled out the cork.

VROOOSH and KAZOOOM! Gonzo found himself standing in the middle of a dress shop that was as large as a circus tent and just as crowded. Everywhere were soft velvet dresses, fancy lace coats, satiny blouses, and delicate scarves made of feathers and frills. At Gonzo's feet lay a long gown and matching cape.

The Martians looked high and low for Gonzo, but they couldn't find him anywhere in the dress shop.

"Which way did he go?" a yellow one asked a pink.

The pink Martian didn't know, but the strange figure in the long cape pointed out the door.

"Thanks for the help," squealed the Martians as they left.

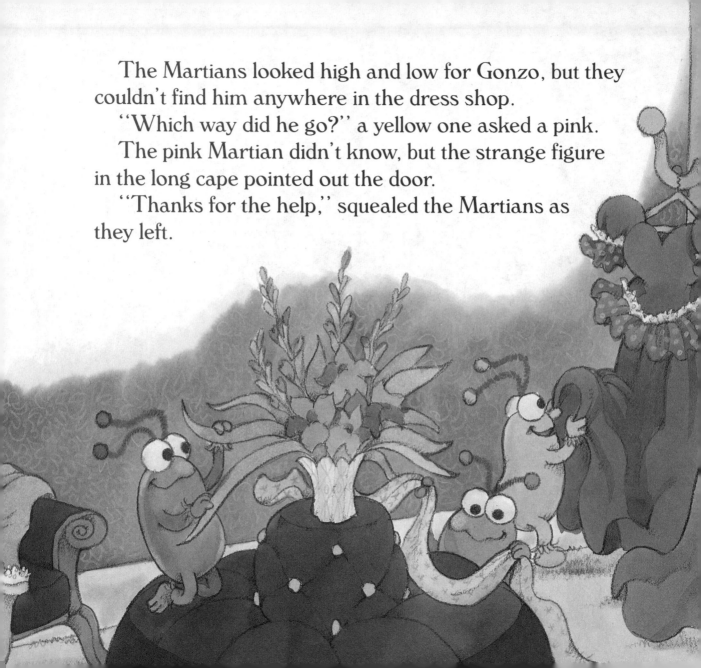

Gonzo watched the Martians climb aboard their flying china saucers. "Should I call them back for another round of tag?" he wondered. But just then, the saucers reminded Gonzo of something. "Yipes!" he gasped. "I may have missed the tea party in the nursery. And I'm hungry."

Gonzo quickly gathered up the three dream bottles and ran back to the flea market. On the way, he noticed that the bottles didn't look empty.

"Thanks for helping me find my unfinished dream,"
Gonzo said to Felicia Flea. Then handing her the three
bottles, he asked, "Don't the dreams in these ever get
used up?"

Felicia's green eyes glittered again. "Here's some more
flea advice," she said. "Remember that a good dream
never ends. You can always come back to it."

Felicia smiled with the wink of a flea.

Gonzo blinked...

...*AND THERE HE WAS*—
back in time for cookies and tea.